Dear Parent:
Your child's love of reading starts here!

Every child learns to read in a different way and at his or her own speed. Some go back and forth between reading levels and read favorite books again and again. Others read through each level in order. You can help your young reader improve and become more confident by encouraging his or her own interests and abilities. From books your child reads with you to the first books he or she reads alone, there are I Can Read Books for every stage of reading:

SHARED READING
Basic language, word repetition, and whimsical illustrations ideal for sharing with your emergent reader

BEGINNING READING
Short sentences, familiar words, and simple concep for children eager to read on their own

READING WITH HELP
Engaging stories, longer sentences, and language pla for developing readers

READING ALONE
Complex plots, challenging vocabulary, and high-interest topics for the independent reader

ADVANCED READING
Short paragraphs, chapters, and exciting themes for the perfect bridge to chapter books

I Can Read Books have introduced children to the joy of reading since 1957. Featuring award-winning authors and illustrators and a fabulous cast of beloved characters, I Can Read Books set the standard for beginning readers.

A lifetime of discovery begins with the magical words **"I Can Read!"**

Visit www.icanread.com for information
on enriching your child's reading experience.

I Can Read Book® is a trademark of HarperCollins Publishers.

Ice Age: Continental Drift: Best Friends
Ice Age: Continental Drift™ & © 2012 Twentieth Century Fox Film Corporation. All rights reserved. Printed in the United States of America. No part of this book may be used or reproduced in any manner whatsoever without written permission except in the case of brief quotations embodied in critical articles and reviews. For information address HarperCollins Children's Books, a division of HarperCollins Publishers, 10 East 53rd Street, New York, NY 10022.
www.icanread.com
Library of Congress catalog number: 2012932728
ISBN 978-0-06-210483-0
Book design by Rick Farley

12 13 14 15 16 LP/WOR 10 9 8 7 6 5 4 3 2 1   ❖   First Edition

www.iceagemovie.com

I Can Read!

READING 2 WITH HELP

ICE AGE
CONTINENTAL DRIFT
BEST FRIENDS

Written by J. E. Bright

HARPER
An Imprint of HarperCollinsPublishers

Everybody needs family and friends and love to survive in the world.

For most of us that means there are people we love in our lives.

But not Scrat.

Scrat only loves his acorn.

He is willing to risk anything

to get a hold of that nut—

even if it means cracking open

a whole continent!

Manny the mammoth, Sid the sloth,

and Diego the saber-toothed tiger

are best friends.

Together they are their own herd.

Even Sid's real family
doesn't stick by him like his friends do.
Manny, Diego, and Sid
are always there for one another.

Manny lost his first family
to human hunters with spears.

Luckily, Manny met Ellie
and fell in love with her.

Ellie was raised by possums

named Crash and Eddie.

Ellie sleeps strangely for a mammoth.

Like a possum, she hangs

from a tree by her tail!

Manny and Ellie have a daughter.

Her name is Peaches.

Peaches loves her parents,

but she is a teenager.

She wants to do things her way.

Sometimes Manny and Peaches fight

about Manny's rules for her.

"You can't control my life!" she yells.

"I'm a dad!" he says. "That's my job!"

Crash and Eddie are brothers.

Before Ellie met Manny,

she thought she was their real sister!

As Peaches's uncles, Crash and Eddie

are supposed to keep an eye on her.

Crash and Eddie are always happy,

even when the world might be ending.

What's their secret?

As Crash says, "We're very stupid."

But they love their mammoth family.

A teen molehog named Louis
is Peaches's best friend.

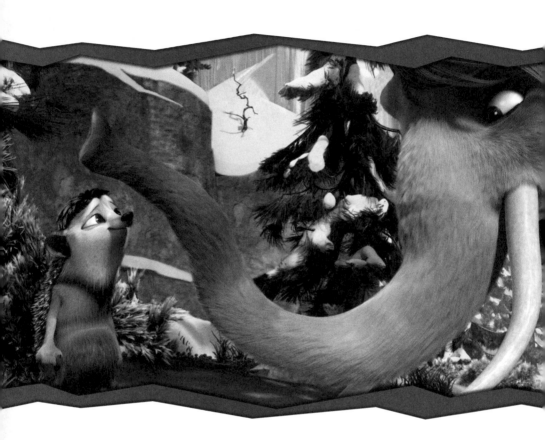

Louis is a bit different,
but he would do anything for Peaches.
He has a big crush on her.

Louis is so loyal,

he helps Peaches sneak out to the Falls.

The Falls is a teen hangout,

and Manny doesn't want her going there.

Peaches has a crush on

a cool teen mammoth named Ethan.

Ethan likes her, too.

By accident, they tangle their tusks.

Manny has to pull them apart.

Ethan tells Peaches that to be cool

she has to stop hanging out with Louis.

Peaches realizes Ethan isn't so cool.

He's not the right mammoth for her.

When the ice shelf breaks,

a crack opens between Manny

and Ellie and Peaches.

The mammoth family gets separated.

"I will find you!" promises Manny.

Manny, Sid, and Diego float away

on a big chunk of ice.

Together they survive a storm,

but they're lost at sea.

"We still have each other," says Sid.

Then they find a stowaway

inside a hollow log.

It's Sid's granny!

Granny is a crazy old sloth.

She has an imaginary friend.

She never bathes.

But Sid is thrilled to have her along.

They see another iceberg
floating toward them!
Sid, Manny, and Diego think
they're being rescued.
But the iceberg is full of pirates!

Captain Gutt is an enormous orangutan.

His first mate is Shira,

a female saber-toothed tiger.

The pirates decide

to battle Manny and his friends!

In the battle, Shira falls overboard,
and Diego rescues her.

Shira is fierce!

Diego and Shira bicker a lot,

but they learn to respect each other.

When the guys battle the pirates again,

Shira's not sure which family to choose.

But she trusts Diego more than Gutt!

Just when it looks like

the pirates might win,

Granny calls for her pet, Precious.

Precious isn't imaginary after all—

he's a gigantic whale!

The pirates are no match for Precious!

Manny reunites with Ellie and Peaches.

He's happy to be back

with his mammoth family.

With their help,

and the help of brave little Louis,

the pirates are defeated.

There's only one major problem—

they can't go back home.

It's unlivable there now.

Luckily, Sid has a great idea.

He gets Precious to push an iceberg

loaded with all the animals

to a beautiful new world!

The animals settle in to their new home

with all their friends and loved ones.

"You've got a nice family here,"

Granny tells Sid. "A *real* family."

"I'm pretty lucky." Sid sighs happily.

Everyone needs something to love
to survive in the world.
Even Scrat.